Mary
the Sharing
Fairy

Join the **Rainbow Magic Reading Challenge!**

Read the story and collect your fairy points to climb the
Reading Rainbow at the back of the book.

This book is worth 5 points.

To Darcie Horne

Special thanks to
Rachel Elliot

ORCHARD BOOKS

First published in Great Britain in 2016 by The Watts Publishing Group

3 5 7 9 10 8 6 4 2

© 2016 Rainbow Magic Limited.
© 2016 HIT Entertainment Limited.
Illustrations © Orchard Books 2016

HIT entertainment

A CIP catalogue record for this book is available from the British Library.

ISBN 978 1 40834 896 3

Printed and bound in Great Britain by Clays Ltd, Elcograf S.p.A

MIX
Paper from
responsible sources
FSC® C104740

The paper and board used in this book are made from wood from responsible sources

Orchard Books
An imprint of Hachette Children's Group
Part of The Watts Publishing Group Limited
Carmelite House, 50 Victoria Embankment, London EC4Y 0DZ

An Hachette UK Company
www.hachette.co.uk
www.hachettechildrens.co.uk

Mary
the Sharing
Fairy

by Daisy Meadows

ORCHARD

www.rainbowmagic.co.uk

Jack Frost's Spell

The Friendship Fairies like big smiles.
They want to spread good cheer for miles.
Those pests want people to connect,
And treat each other with respect.

I don't agree! I just don't care!
I want them all to feel despair.
And when their charms belong to me,
Each friend will be an enemy!

Contents

Painting Plans

"I can't wait to find out what we'll be doing in the Summer Friends Club today," said Kirsty Tate.

She grinned at her best friend, Rachel Walker, who was bouncing up and down on a space hopper. They were inside a brightly coloured tepee tent in Rainspell Park, where the holiday club was based.

"Whatever it is, I'm sure it'll be fun," said Rachel, her blonde curls flying around her head as she bounced. "We'll be together!"

Rachel and Kirsty had been friends ever since their first meeting on Rainspell Island. It was an extra-special place for them because they had also become friends with the fairies during that first holiday.

This time they were staying at the Sunny Days Bed and Breakfast with their parents. They had joined the Summer Friends Club on their first day, and were excited to find that the teenage girls who ran it, Ginny and Jen, were best friends too. Today was their second day, and they were both looking forward to finding out what Ginny and Jen had planned.

The tepee was already ringing with laughter. Oscar and Lara, who they had met the previous day, were practising one-handed cartwheels. When they collapsed to the ground, out of breath and giggling, Rachel and Kirsty came over to join them.

"Good morning!" said Lara in a
cheerful voice. "It's great to see you here
again. We're really looking forward to
today."

"Us too," said Kirsty. "We were just
wondering what we'll be doing."

"Wonder no more!" said Ginny's
friendly voice behind them. "We've got
something really
awesome planned
for today."

The children
looked
around
and saw
Ginny and
Jen standing
in the tent
entrance, arm in

arm. Several other children crowded in around them.

"We're going to paint a mural on the tennis clubhouse," said Jen, giving a little hop of excitement. "I'm so thrilled that we've got the chance to do this. I know you're all super-creative, and we're going to make the best mural ever."

Chattering and giggling, Rachel and Kirsty headed off across the park with the others. The clubhouse stood at the entrance to the tennis courts, and Jen and Ginny led everyone around to the back. They saw a small picnic area on wooden decking, and Jen pointed at the long side wall of the clubhouse.

"This is the wall we're going to paint," she said. "They want us to brighten up the picnic area."

"What are we going to paint?" asked Oscar.

"The theme of the mural is 'Friendship'," said Ginny. "We thought that we could start by painting the word 'Friendship' on the wall. Then we can decorate it."

Jen took out a big book filled with letters and patterns.

"This book has tons of ideas for lettering styles and decorations for the mural," she said.

She handed the book to Oscar while Ginny passed around the painting aprons. Kirsty and Rachel exchanged a big smile.

"A friendship mural," said Rachel in a low voice. "That's perfect."

"I can't wait to get started," said Kirsty.

Ginny and Jen went to get the paints and brushes from a shed at the side of the picnic area, and Rachel and Kirsty put on their painting aprons.

But, suddenly, Kirsty felt someone tugging at her apron. She turned and saw a girl called Amy frowning at her.

"You've got the best apron," said Amy. "Why should *you* have it?"

Kirsty looked down at her apron in confusion.

"But mine's exactly the same as yours," she said.

"Give it to me!" said Amy.

Shrugging, but wanting to keep the peace, Kirsty handed her apron to Amy and picked up another one. Amy glared at her.

"You're keeping all the best ones for

yourself," she exclaimed. "That's mean."

"Kirsty is *not* mean!" Rachel cried,
stepping forward to defend Kirsty.

But Amy had already turned away to
argue about aprons with someone else.

Rachel and Kirsty went over to the
picnic table, where Oscar was poring
over the ideas book.

"Could we have a look, too?" asked
Rachel.

"Wait your turn," muttered Oscar.

Rachel and Kirsty looked at each other.
Why were the other children suddenly
being so selfish?

Faulty Friendships

Suddenly, Oscar gave a yell. A boy called Eric had snatched the book from him.

"Give it back!" Oscar cried.

"You're not sharing!" Eric retorted. "It's my turn now."

Just then, Jen and Ginny came back, their arms filled with paintbrushes and tins of paint.

"Now we can get on with the fun of painting," said Kirsty.

But no one heard her – they were too busy arguing.

"Stop taking all the good brushes!" Amy was saying at the top of her voice. "*I* should have the best ones."

"I want the green paint," said Eric.

"No, *I* want it!" Oscar yelled, grabbing the tin of paint and trying to wrestle it away from Eric.

Meanwhile, Lara had already started painting and had almost finished the 'f' of the word 'Friendship' in red.

"Wait!" Amy wailed. "That's not fair! *Everyone* was supposed to help write the word. *I* wanted to write the 'f'. I wanted to do it in purple!"

"Come on," said Oscar, grabbing a paintbrush. "Let's help to finish it."

Kirsty and Rachel joined him and they started to paint.

"Hey!" said Lara. "Oscar is *my* best friend, so he should paint with *me*, not you!"

She glared at Kirsty and Rachel and dragged Oscar away from them. The girls looked at Ginny and Jen, hoping that they would sort things out. But the teenagers weren't looking at the children. They were each holding on tight to one end of a tennis racquet, and they were both red in the face.

"I should have the racquet," said Ginny. "The Rainspell Park Committee gave it as a thank you for painting the wall, and painting it was my idea."

"No, it wasn't!" Jen exclaimed. "I thought of it first, and I was the one who got permission from the Park Committee, so *I* should have the tennis racquet."

"But I organised all the paints and supplies," Ginny said, through gritted teeth. "This racquet should be mine."

Kirsty and Rachel exchanged a worried glance.

"I can't believe that they're fighting like this," said Rachel. "They're supposed to be best friends."

Kirsty looked around at the other children. They were all arguing now. Even Oscar and Lara were snatching paintbrushes out of each other's hands.

"Nobody wants to share anything," Kirsty said. "This is all because of Jack Frost and his pesky goblins. None of them understands what true friendship is."

Jack Frost's troublemaking ways were fresh in their memory. Just the day before, the Friendship Fairies had invited Rachel and Kirsty to a tea party in Fairyland. The girls had been having a lovely time with Esther the Kindness Fairy, Mary the Sharing Fairy, Mimi the Laughter Fairy and Clare the Caring Fairy – until Jack Frost and the goblins had snuck into the garden and stolen their magical objects!

Jack Frost had taken the magical objects so that he could be super-powerful with lots of friends to boss around. He had ordered the goblins to take the magical objects to the human world and find some friends for him.

Remembering the shocked faces of the Friendship Fairies, Rachel felt more determined than ever to get the magical objects back.

"All these friendships should be strong and happy," she said, looking around at the other children. "Without the magical objects, they're all going to be in ruins. We have to help all the Friendship Fairies get their things back."

Watching Ginny and Jen, Kirsty felt tears of sympathy prickling her eyes. She thought about how horrible it would feel to argue with Rachel like that. Luckily, their old friend Florence the Friendship Fairy had cast a 'Friends Through Thick and Thin' spell on their bracelets, so their friendship wouldn't be affected. But

Florence's spell wouldn't last for ever. If the fairies didn't get their objects back soon, even Rachel and Kirsty would turn against each other.

Rachel guessed what Kirsty was thinking and squeezed her hand.

"We helped Esther the Kindness Fairy to get her magical heart brooch back from the goblins yesterday," she said. "We can do this, don't worry."

"It just seems like such a huge task," said Kirsty. "If we don't find the three remaining missing magical objects, *all* friendships will be ruined. People can't fight about every little thing and then still be best friends at the end of it all."

Suddenly, there was a yell from the children beside the picnic table. Amy and Eric were covered in orange paint, which was also spilling all across the decking.

"That was your fault!" Amy snapped.

"No, you spilled it," Eric replied.

"Things are getting worse," said Rachel with a groan. "This is awful!"

Magic in a Mop Bucket

Jen and Ginny were so involved in their argument over the tennis racquet that they hadn't noticed the spillage.

"Let's go and get a mop and bucket," said Rachel. "I don't think anyone else is going to clean it up. They're much too busy squabbling."

The girls made their way over to the shed and stepped inside. It took their eyes a few moments to adjust to being out of the bright sunshine. Then Rachel pointed to a far corner.

"There's a bucket," she said. "And there's a mop sticking out of it."

Kirsty stepped forward and picked up the mop. At once there was a tiny burst of sparkles, and then Mary the Sharing Fairy fluttered out of the mop bucket.

Mary was wearing white skinny jeans, sparkly gold sandals and a folk-patterned pink T-shirt. The charm bracelets around her wrist rattled as she waved at the girls, but they knew that the most important charm of all was missing.

"Hello, Rachel and Kirsty!" Mary said in an eager voice. "I'm so happy that you came in here. I'm determined to find my magical yin and yang charm today, and I'm hoping that you might be able to help me."

"Of course we'll help you," said Kirsty. "We've just seen how horrible things are when friends don't share. It's spoiling everything that Jen and Ginny had planned."

Mary shook back her loose blonde hair and her eyes sparkled behind her glasses.

"I'm sure that by working together, we'll be able to get the charm back," she said. "I believe that sharing really matters, and that means sharing trouble as well as sharing fun. With you two to help me, how can we fail?"

Rachel was remembering the tiny black-and-white charm that she had seen dangling from Mary's wrist when they had first met.

"What do the yin and yang symbols mean?" she asked.

"Yin and yang are two halves that make a whole when you put them together," said Mary.

"Just like friends," said Kirsty, with a smile. "When two people work together, they can make a whole, true friendship."

"Exactly right," Mary replied. "Now, all three of us need to work together to find the missing charm and help people to be able to share again. Let's go!"

Mary flew into the pocket of Kirsty's painting apron, and then the girls went out of the shed, carrying the mop and bucket.

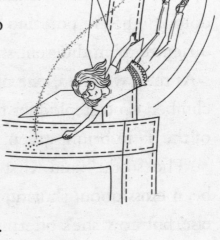

There was no one on the decking now
– the children were all crowding around
the mural.

As Rachel and Kirsty cleaned up the
spilled paint, they saw that a new group
of boys was standing among the other
children in the Summer Friends Club.
They were all wearing green aprons and
matching painting caps.

"Look," said Rachel, standing up on
tiptoe to see what the new boys were
doing. "They're painting the 'F' of
'Friendship' in different shades of green."

As they watched, one of the boys
climbed up a stepladder to paint the top
of the 'F' in bright green.

"That's odd," said Kirsty. "Amy has
been cross about sharing with anyone
else, but now she's offering to share her

purple paint with that boy on the ladder.
The others are holding up their paints,
too."

Rachel and Kirsty walked closer to the
others, just as the boy on the ladder blew
a raspberry at Amy.

"We only like painting in green," he snapped. "Take that yucky purple away."

Rachel drew in her breath sharply. Under the boy's green painting cap, she caught a glimpse of a long green nose.

"Those aren't boys," she said to Kirsty in a low voice. "They're goblins! They must have Mary's magical object."

"But which one of them has it?" Kirsty asked.

"It must be the one on the ladder," said Rachel. "Everyone wants to share with him."

Just then, Jen handed the goblin another tin of green paint.

"How about painting the rest of the mural in a different colour?" she suggested.

The goblin simply grunted at her. Jen set the other children to work further down the wall on the rest of the mural. They all still seemed more interested in arguing than in painting, but for now they weren't paying attention to the goblins.

"I've got an idea!" said Rachel.

Tennis Trouble

Rachel leaned down to whisper into the pocket of Kirsty's apron. "Mary, could you use your magic to change the colour of the paint in the goblins' tins?" she asked.

She couldn't even see the little fairy, but the tip of Mary's wand poked out of the top of the pocket, and the girls heard

Mary's silvery voice speaking the words of a spell.

"*Rainbow Fairies, hear my plea,*
Lend your colour spells to me.
Change the paint before their eyes
To a colour they despise."

Mary's wand tip waved, a flash of rainbow sparkles burst from it, and in an instant the green paint that the goblins were using turned bright pink!

"Urgh!" shouted the goblin on the ladder. "Revolting! Give me a new tin!"

One of the goblins opened another green tin, but the paint inside was also bright pink.

"What a load of rubbish!" the goblin on the ladder squawked. "What's wrong with this paint?"

Kirsty and Rachel stepped forward.

"Nothing's wrong with it," said Kirsty.
"You can have the green paint back
as soon as you return Mary's magical
charm. All you have to do is give
something back that doesn't belong to
you in the first place."

"It's the right thing to do," Rachel
added seriously.

But the goblins curled their lips, narrowed their eyes and wrinkled up their noses as if they had smelled something bad.

"There's no way you're getting this back," said the goblin on the ladder. He held up his arm and jingled the bracelet he was wearing. Mary's yin and yang charm was dangling from it.

"It's mine now, and I'm keeping it," he added. "Now leave us alone!"

With that, the goblin jumped down from the ladder and raced off towards the tennis courts, closely followed by the other goblins.

43

"It'll be easier to follow them as fairies,"
said Rachel. "Mary, will you use your
magic to transform us both?"

"With pleasure!" said Mary.

The girls darted around the corner
of the clubhouse, out of sight of the
other children. Then Mary popped out
of Kirsty's apron pocket and hovered in
front of them both, holding her wand
high above her head.

"We have to save my yin-yang charm,
Before more friendships suffer harm.
Untie these painting apron strings,
And lend my friends their fairy wings!"

Rachel and Kirsty felt something
magically pulling at them, and then the
aprons they were wearing were whisked
away. In the twinkling of an eye they
had shrunk into tiny fairies, their wings

shimmering like mother-of-pearl as they
rose into the air beside Mary.

"They're heading towards the tennis
courts," said Kirsty. "Come on, let's follow
them."

Two people were playing a tennis
match when the goblins ran onto the
court. One of the players was distracted
and hit the ball out, but she didn't seem
to mind. Instead, she jogged over to the
goblin with the yin and yang charm and
handed him her racquet.

"Would you like to play now?" she asked him. "It only seems fair that we should share so that you get a turn, too."

The goblin snatched the racquet from her without saying thank you, while the other goblins argued over the second player's racquet. The players walked off towards the clubhouse.

The goblin with the charm picked up a tennis ball and threw it into the air a couple of times, catching it as it came down. He gazed around and saw the fairies hovering beside the net. A mean smile flickered around his mouth. Then he hit the ball at the fairies as hard as he could. Rachel, Kirsty and Mary dived in opposite directions. Quick as a flash,

he launched another ball at them, and another, and another. The fairies dodged left and right – it was all they could do to stay safe and keep away from the speeding tennis balls.

"There's no way we can get close to the charm while he's hitting balls at us," said Mary, panting. "Maybe we should leave and try again later."

Kirsty shook her head, but before she could reply she saw another tennis ball heading directly towards her. She darted sideways to avoid it, but she wasn't looking where she was going. *Crash!* She flew straight into the net that divided the tennis court!

Goblin in a Spin

In a tangle of arms, legs and wings, Kirsty struggled to free herself. Rachel zoomed down to help.

"Are you OK?" Rachel asked, giving her a hug.

"I'm fine," said Kirsty, bubbling with excitement. "It's given me an idea that I really think might work!"

She told Rachel and Mary her plan, and then the three of them took their positions. The other goblins were still arguing when Rachel and Kirsty flew towards the goblin with the charm.

"I don't think you can hit us with those tennis balls," said Rachel in a loud voice. "Your aim isn't good enough."

"My aim is perfect!" the goblin squeaked. "You'd better get out of the way or I'll flatten you both like pancakes!"

"Oh, no, you won't," said Kirsty, with a laugh. "You're not quick enough."

Carefully, so that the goblin didn't even realise it was happening, Rachel and Kirsty led him closer to the net. He flung more balls at them, but they simply dodged them and laughed, until the goblin grew so angry that his eyes nearly popped out of his head.

"Stay still!" he hissed, stepping still closer to the net.

Rachel glanced sideways and saw Mary hiding beside the net. The Sharing Fairy held up one finger, meaning that she needed Jack Frost to come just one step closer.

Rachel and Kirsty fluttered backwards.

"I've seen tennis balls being hit much harder and faster than this," said Rachel.

53

With a yell of rage, the goblin took
another step forwards. Then Mary waved
her wand, and the tennis net flung itself
into the air
and wound itself
around the goblin,
rolling him up in
it like a mummy.
Within seconds,
all that could
be seen of the
goblin was
his angry
face and his
enormous
feet.

"Grrr!" he said,
baring his teeth at the fairies. "Let me go,
you flying pests!"

"You know what we want," said Mary. "Give me my charm and I will let you go."

"I'll share some tennis balls with you," the goblin offered. "You can even use my racquet."

"The charm," said Rachel, folding her arms across her chest.

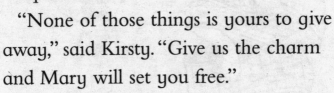

"I'll let you *have* all the tennis balls!" the goblin exclaimed. "And you can *keep* both racquets!"

"None of those things is yours to give away," said Kirsty. "Give us the charm and Mary will set you free."

"I don't believe you," the goblin said, looking grumpy.

"Kirsty and I never tell lies, and neither do the fairies," said Rachel. "You can trust us to keep our promises."

"You can take all the other goblins prisoner!" shouted the goblin, sounding desperate now. "You can lock them in

dungeons and feed them on mouldy bread!"

"We don't have dungeons in Fairyland, and I don't want prisoners," said Mary. "There is only one thing I want – the charm that you and Jack Frost stole from me. Give it back, and things will return to normal."

"What if I don't like 'normal'?" the goblin wailed.

"Then change it," said Kirsty. "You don't *have* to do everything that Jack Frost says, you know."

The goblin closed his eyes and pulled a horrible face. Then he opened his eyes again.

"Fine," he said. "I guess you three don't care how much trouble I'm going to get into about this."

The fairies didn't reply, but they watched as the goblin wriggled and jiggled about on the spot. It wasn't easy, because his arms were pressed tightly against his sides, but at last there was a tinkling sound as something fell out of the bottom of the tennis-net wrap.

The fairies dived towards it and saw the precious yin and yang charm. The goblin had managed to unhook it.

"At last!" said Mary, picking up the charm, which shrank to fairy size. "Oh, I was starting to worry that I would never get it back!"

She hooked it to her bracelet and tapped the tennis net with her wand. Immediately, it unwound itself at top speed, sending the goblin staggering dizzily across the tennis court towards the other goblins.

He crashed into them and they all fell
down together like skittles.

The tennis net returned to its usual
position, and the fairies saw the goblins
start to chew their fingernails.

"Jack Frost is going to be so cross with
us," said one.

"That's two magical objects we've lost now," said another. "He'll be hopping mad! What are we going to do?"

Making Amends

The goblins looked so worried that the fairies felt sorry for them. Mary waved her wand and magical red-and-white sparkles erupted into the air like a fountain.

"*Even if they steal and pout,*
I don't like leaving people out.
For I believe it's only fair,
That everyone has treats to share."

In front of the goblins' eyes, the red
sparkles tumbled into a large china bowl
and became strawberries, while the
white sparkles poured themselves into a
big jug and became cream. The goblins
were delighted! They forgot their worries
as they tucked in, gobbling so fast that
bright red strawberry juice trickled down
their chins.

Laughing, the fairies turned to each other and shared a big, happy hug.

"You two have been so amazing," Mary told Rachel and Kirsty. "I've heard about what good friends you are, of course, but you're even more wonderful than I could have imagined. You're just like my yin and yang charm – you belong together."

As they hugged, the girls felt themselves growing and their wings disappearing. Then they were back to their usual size, and Mary was hovering in front of them.

"Goodbye!" she said, waving and smiling at them. "I hope we'll meet again soon!"

She disappeared in a starry swoosh of fairy dust, and the girls reached for each other's hand.

"Come on!" said Rachel. "Let's go and see how the others are getting on now that the charm is back where it belongs."

They raced back to the wall at the back of the tennis clubhouse, and found Ginny, Jen and the children gazing sadly at the mural. After all the arguments, paint splashes and goblin interference, the wall was a mess.

"What are we going to do?" asked Amy.

Eric bent down and picked up the ideas book. It fell open at a colourful page, and a little smile appeared on his face.

"Look at this, everyone," he said, holding out the book so that they could all share it. "I think we might be able to fix it if we try this."

"Oh, yes, what a good idea!" said Ginny. "It might work really well with the idea on page fifty."

They turned to the right page and agreed exactly what they would do. Then, working together and sharing the paint and paintbrushes between them, the children  repainted and decorated the word 'Friendship' on the wall. Kirsty painted one of the letters with Oscar, while Rachel painted with Lara.

"It's fun sharing friends, isn't it?" said Lara.

Rachel smiled back at her, feeling happy that Lara was back to her normal, friendly self.

While they painted, the girls noticed Ginny and Jen chatting about what to do with the tennis racquet. They had been arguing about it earlier, but now they were full of smiles.

"You should have it, Ginny," said Jen. "You deserve it more than I do."

"No way," said Ginny. "It's all yours."

Kirsty grinned at Rachel and then leaned over to the teenagers.

"Why don't you share it?" she suggested. "You could take turns using it to play, or bouncing a tennis ball on it!"

They exchanged a glance and nodded.

"That's the perfect solution," said Ginny. "Why didn't we think of it?"

Kirsty and Rachel knew why! But, of course, they could never tell anyone about their fairy adventures, so they just shared a secret smile.

Later, when the mural was finished

and looking brilliant, the children helped
Ginny and Jen clean all the brushes and
tidy the paint tins away. It was hot work
in the sunshine, but everyone was glad to
help.

Rachel and Kirsty said goodbye to
the others and headed back to the bed
and breakfast. On the way, they spotted
the Rainspell Island ice-cream stall,
which was run by a friendly lady called
Heather.

"Are you thinking what I'm thinking?"
Rachel asked her best friend, with a grin.

"Definitely!" said Kirsty.

They bought an ice-cream cone to
share and took it in turns to have a lick
as they walked along.

"Sharing is something we do all the
time as best friends, isn't it?" said Rachel,

as Kirsty caught a drip of strawberry ice cream with her tongue. "I'm so glad that we found Mary's magical charm."

"Me, too," said Kirsty, handing the cone to Rachel. "Now all friends will remember to share. But friendships aren't quite safe yet. We have to find the two missing magical objects for the Friendship Fairies. I hope we get the chance to help them very soon."

"Tomorrow is a brand-new day," said Rachel, smiling at Kirsty. "And I'm sure that it'll bring us a brand-new adventure with our fairy friends!"

The End

Now it's time for Kirsty and
Rachel to help...

Mimi the Laughter Fairy

Read on for a sneak peek...

Kirsty Tate was spinning her way across
the park, her arms outstretched as she
soaked up the early morning sunshine.
It was making the dew sparkle on each
blade of grass, and it was shining on the
golden hair of Kirsty's best friend,
Rachel Walker.

"I wonder what Jen and Ginny have
planned for us today," said Rachel,
skipping along beside Kirsty.

It was their third day on Rainspell
Island, the beautiful place where they had
first met – and where they'd had their
first fairy adventure! They had joined

the Summer Friends Club, a holiday play scheme for children staying on the island, and the club met in the park every morning.

"We've already played football, had a water-balloon fight and painted a mural," Kirsty remembered. "I'm so glad we joined the club."

They reached the tepee-style tent where the club was based and stepped inside. Oscar and Lara, two of their newest friends, dashed over to them.

"Good morning!" said Lara, a big smile on her face.

"Do you know what we're doing today?" Oscar asked.

"We have no idea," said Rachel, with a grin. "It looks as if we're about to find out, though!"

Jen and Ginny, the teenage best

friends who ran the club, were beckoning everyone to gather around them. They looked as if they were about to burst with excitement.

"Today we have something really fantastic for you all to enjoy," said Ginny. "We're going to watch a special performance by Mr Twinkle himself!"

Read **Mimi the Laughter Fairy** to find out what adventures are in store for Kirsty and Rachel!

Competition!

The Friendship Fairies have created a special
competition just for you!

Collect all four books in the Friendship Fairies series
and answer the special questions in the back of each one.

Who does Eric have a paint fight with?

— — —

Once you have all four answers, take the first letter from
each one and arrange them to spell a secret word!
When you have the answer, go online and enter!

We will put all the correct entries into a draw and select
a winner to receive a special Rainbow Magic Goody Bag
featuring lots of treats for you and your fairy friends.
The winner will also feature in a new Rainbow Magic story!

Enter online now at www.rainbowmagicbooks.co.uk

Calling all parents, carers and teachers!
The Rainbow Magic fairies are here to help
your child enter the magical world of reading.
Whatever reading stage they are at, there's
a Rainbow Magic book for everyone!
Here is Lydia the Reading Fairy's guide to
supporting your child's journey at all levels.

Starting Out

1 Our Rainbow Magic Beginner Readers are perfect for first-time readers who are just beginning to develop reading skills and confidence. Approved by teachers, they contain a full range of educational levelling, as well as lively full-colour illustrations.

Developing Readers

2 Rainbow Magic Early Readers contain longer stories and wider vocabulary for building stamina and growing confidence. These are adaptations of our most popular Rainbow Magic stories, specially developed for younger readers in conjunction with an Early Years reading consultant, with full-colour illustrations.

Going Solo

3 The Rainbow Magic chapter books - a mixture of series and one-off specials - contain accessible writing to encourage your child to venture into reading independently. These highly collectible and much-loved magical stories inspire a love of reading to last a lifetime.

www.rainbowmagicbooks.co.uk

"Rainbow Magic got my daughter reading chapter books. Great sparkly covers, cute fairies and traditional stories full of magic that she found impossible to put down" - Mother of Edie (6 years)

"Florence LOVES the Rainbow Magic books. She really enjoys reading now" Mother of Florence (6 years)

The Rainbow Magic Reading Challenge

Well done, fairy friend – you have completed the book!
This book was worth 5 points.

See how far you have climbed on the **Reading Rainbow**
on the Rainbow Magic website below.

The more books you read, the more points you will get,
and the closer you will be to becoming a Fairy Princess!

How to get your Reading Rainbow
1. Cut out the coin below
2. Go to the Rainbow Magic website
3. Download and print out your poster
4. Add your coin and climb up the Reading Rainbow!

There's all this and lots more at
www.rainbowmagicbooks.co.uk

You'll find activities, competitions, stories, a special
newsletter and complete profiles of all the
Rainbow Magic fairies. Find a fairy with your name!